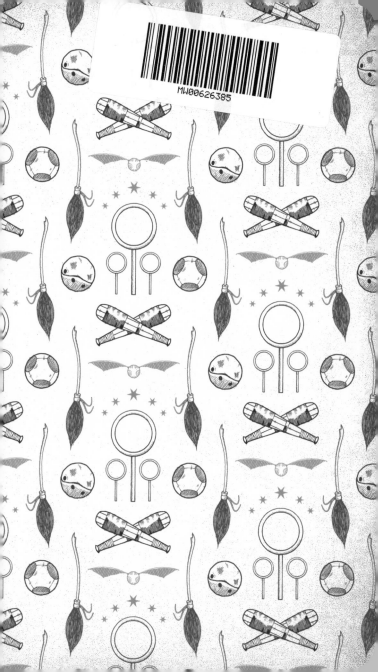

MW00626385

FROM THE FILMS OF

Harry Potter

QUIDDITCH
— AT —
HOGWARTS

THE FAN'S JOURNAL

DONALD LEMKE

RUNNING PRESS
PHILADELPHIA

Running Press
Hachette Book Group
1290 Avenue of the Americas, New York, NY 10104
www.runningpress.com
@Running_Press

Printed in China

First Edition: April 2020

Published by Running Press, an imprint of Perseus Books, LLC, a
subsidiary of Hachette Book Group, Inc. The Running Press name
and logo is a trademark of the Hachette Book Group.

The Hachette Speakers Bureau provides a wide range of
authors for speaking events. To find out more, go to
www.hachettespeakersbureau.com or call (866) 376-6591.

The publisher is not responsible for websites (or their content)
that are not owned by the publisher.

Print book cover and interior design by Jenna McBride.

Library of Congress Control Number: 2019950927

ISBN: 978-0-7624-6945-1

L-REX

10 9 8 7 6 5 4 3 2 1

CONTENTS

From rivalries at Hogwarts School of Witchcraft and Wizardry to professional showdowns at the Quidditch World Cup, Quidditch is a major part of wizarding life—and a big part of the Harry Potter films. Filmmakers had to rely on the vision and collaboration of many creative people to bring the fast-moving game to life on the big screen.

★ ★ ★

"ROUGH GAME, QUIDDITCH."

—George Weasley,
Harry Potter and the Sorcerer's Stone

In *Harry Potter and the Prisoner of Azkaban*, Harry Potter (Daniel Radcliffe) flies atop his broomstick during a match between Gryffindor and Hufflepuff.

PART ONE

THE PITCH

Quidditch is easy enough to understand," describes Oliver Wood (Sean Biggerstaff) in *Harry Potter and the Sorcerer's Stone*.

THE PITCH

Tall towers and stands ring the Quidditch pitch at Hogwarts, giving fans a bird's-eye view of the match.

According to Stuart Craig, the production designer on all the Harry Potter films, "The pitch was huge, so we couldn't possibly fit it in any stage at the studio. It could fit on the back lot, but there wasn't much point, since the background needed to be the Highlands of Scotland. And of course, it would have been hugely expensive and inconvenient to go and build it in Scotland, so it became one of our first almost entirely computer-generated sets."

GOALPOSTS

The Hogwarts Quidditch pitch sits in the shadow of Hogwarts Castle. Goalposts of varying heights and sizes tower above the pitch, ready for the next match.

In *Harry Potter and the Prisoner of Azkaban*, lightning strikes the goalposts on the Hogwarts Quidditch pitch. The match between Gryffindor and Hufflepuff continued despite the severe weather.

As the films continued, the game became more intense. For *Harry Potter and the Half-Blood Prince*, Stuart Craig re-created the stadium for "super-deluxe Quidditch." More towers were added and were heightened. The bleachers were reconfigured from one basic box to tiered stands. He notes, "By introducing more towers, there were more opportunities for weaving in and out of them, and more things whizzing by in close proximity gives a greater sense of speed."

QUIDDITCH MAGICAL FILM MOMENTS

I n *Harry Potter and the Half-Blood Prince*, Ron Weasley (Rupert Grint) and Cormac McLaggen (Freddie Stroma) faced off for the position of Gryffindor's Keeper. As Cormac blocked Quaffle after Quaffle, Hermione Granger (Emma Watson) secretly whispered *Confundo*, momentarily confusing Cormac and allowing a ball to pass through the hoop. The misstep allowed Ron to win the Keeper position.

Tally the final score between your favorite
Hogwarts Quidditch teams.

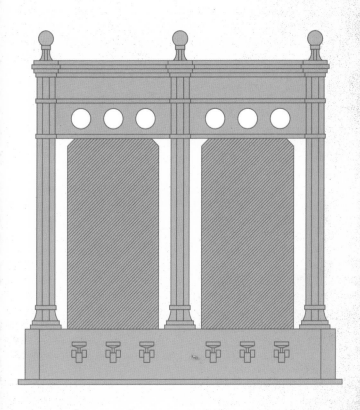

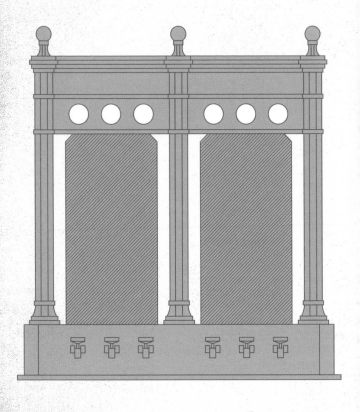

PART TWO

EQUIPMENT & UNIFORMS

Quidditch requires several magical pieces of equipment, including enchanted balls, bats, and—most importantly—broomsticks.

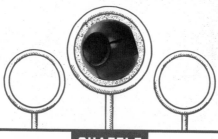

QUAFFLE

As Oliver Wood explains in *Harry Potter and the Sorcerer's Stone*, "There are three kinds of balls," including the Quaffle. Chasers handle the Quaffle and try to put it through the hoops. The four Quaffles created for the films had a red-leather cover wrapped over a core of foam. The stitching was concealed and a Hogwarts crest logo was debossed on the opposite side of the ball.

In *Harry Potter and the Half-Blood Prince*, Ron Weasley celebrates after blocking a Quaffle from going through the hoop.

BLUDGERS

In *Harry Potter and the Chamber of Secrets*, Harry Potter recovers after being struck by a rogue Bludger. Oliver Wood described these balls as, "Nasty little buggers," and for good reason. Each ball used in Quidditch needed to have its own sound as it flew through the air. The sound designers decided that the Bludgers should sound like an angry animal when stuck.

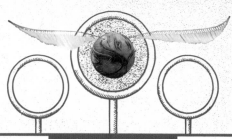

GOLDEN SNITCH

In the words of Oliver Wood, "It's wicked fast and darn near impossible to see." Catching the Golden Snitch results in 150 points, and the game is over. For the Harry Potter films, various designs were considered for both the wings and the body of the Golden Snitch. The final prop included thin, ribbed wings that were sail-shaped attached to a Art-Nouveau style body.

QUIDDITCH MAGICAL
FILM MOMENTS

✦ ✳ ✦

As an all-star Seeker, Harry Potter has a long history of Snitch-catching moments—but perhaps none greater than his first for Gryffindor. In a match versus Slytherin, Harry made a game-winning play that was simply, well . . . *breathtaking*.

GAME ON!

Describe your favorite Snitch-catching moments from the Harry Potter films.

_____

_____

_____

_____

_____

_____

_____

_____

_____

_____

_____

_____

_____

_____

_____

_____

_____

BROOMSTICKS

For a sport played 50 feet in the air, a flying broomstick is undoubtedly the most important piece of Quidditch equipment. For the Harry Potter films, prop designer Pierre Bohanna explains, "The brooms weren't just props that the kids carry around. They have to sit on them. They have to be mounted onto motion-control bases for special effects shots, and twisted and turned to imitate flying, so they had to be very thin and incredibly durable."

---
* * *

"THOSE ARE NIMBUS TWO-THOUSAND AND ONES!"

—Ron Weasley,
Harry Potter and the Chamber of Secrets

In *Harry Potter and the Chamber of Secrets*, Harry Potter chases the Golden Snitch atop his Nimbus 2000. Slytherin rival Draco Malfoy (Tom Felton) follows closely behind, flying on his brand-new Nimbus 2001.

All the Quidditch scenes were filmed in front of a blue or green screen. Chris Columbus, the director on the first two Harry Potter films, noted that without anything to interact with, filming the Quidditch scenes was "one of the most gruelling experiences for the actors." He adds, "Riding the brooms was a tremendously difficult thing, but to create a sense of movement, a sense of urgency, and, at the same time, to feel as if there were real athletes playing a game, was the biggest challenge."

★ ★ ★

"THAT'S NOT JUST A BROOMSTICK, HARRY. IT'S A NIMBUS 2000!"

—Ron Weasley,
Harry Potter and the Sorcerer's Stone

In *Harry Potter and the Prisoner of Azkaban,* Harry receives the gift of a Firebolt broomstick from his godfather, Sirius Black (Gary Oldman). As Fred and George Weasley (James and Oliver Phelps) describe, the Firebolt is "the fastest broom in the world."

Customize these broomsticks for a high-flying advantage on the Quidditch pitch.

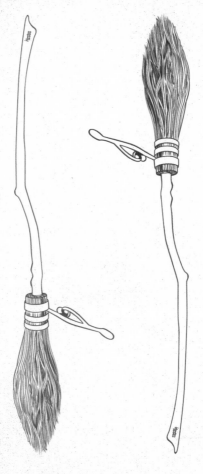

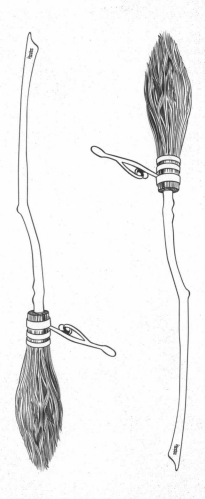

QUIDDITCH MAGICAL FILM MOMENTS

* * *

I n Harry Potter's third year, during a match versus Hufflepuff, Harry chases the Golden Snitch into dark, swirling storm clouds. Moments later, Dementors appear, causing Harry to fall from the sky and break his broomstick in two pieces.

★ ★ ★

"ROUGH GAME, QUIDDITCH. BRUTAL.
BUT NOBODY'S DIED IN YEARS."

—Fred Weasley,
Harry Potter and the Sorcerer's Stone

Team captain Oliver Wood wears Gryffindor's uniform, designed by Judianna Makovsky for *Harry Potter and the Sorcerer's Stone* and *Harry Potter and the Chamber of Secrets*. The uniform features a long, flowing robe, leather arm and shin guards, and team colors.

Keeper Ron Weasley wears Gryffindor's uniform from *Harry Potter and the Half-Blood Prince*. To modernize the uniform, costume designer Jany Temime added stripes and numbers, describing the update as "much more alive and reachable for a teenager."

QUIDDITCH MAGICAL FILM MOMENTS

* ✦ *

In *Harry Potter and the Chamber of Secrets*, rivals Harry Potter and Draco Malfoy race for the Golden Snitch during a Gryffindor versus Slytherin Quidditch match. In the back-and-forth chase, a rogue Bludger injures both players, but Harry still manages to capture the Snitch—and victory.

Design your own Hogwarts Quidditch uniform
to withstand the dangers of the sport.

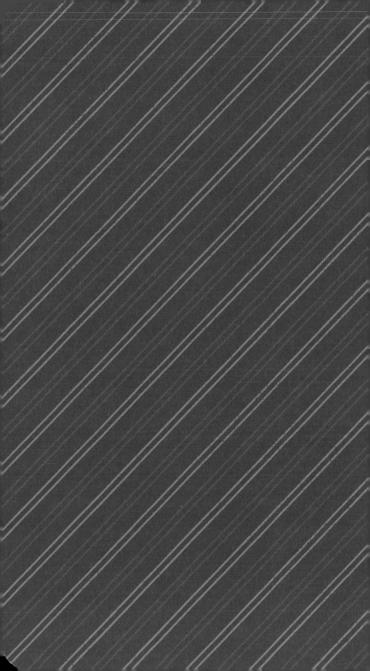

PART THREE

BADGES
& BANNERS

At Hogwarts, Quidditch fans cheer on Gryffindor, waving flags and wearing the colors of their favorite team.

* * *

"HARRY POTTER HAS CAUGHT THE SNITCH! GRYFFINDOR WINS!"

—Lee Jordan, *Harry Potter and the Chamber of Secrets*

GRYFFINDOR SPIRIT

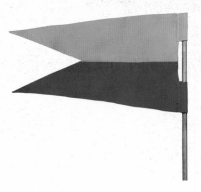

OFFICIAL COLORS: RED AND GOLD

---★---

MASCOT: LION

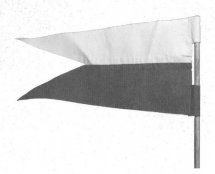

OFFICIAL COLORS: BLUE AND BRONZE

—— ★ ——

MASCOT: EAGLE

KING (OR QUEEN) OF THE FANS

No fan is more dedicated than Luna Lovegood. Her giant lion hat is a sight to see—and be seen—with animated facial expressions, blinking eyes, and a cheerful roar. Actress Evanna Lynch, who portrayed Luna, drew a concept drawing for the costume designers while they were creating Luna's hat. She said she "wanted it to look like it was eating her head."

SLYTHERIN SPIRIT

OFFICIAL COLORS: GREEN AND SILVER

★

MASCOT: SERPENT

OFFICIAL COLORS: YELLOW AND BLACK

---★---

MASCOT: BADGER

Design a badge and banner to show your
Quidditch school spirit.

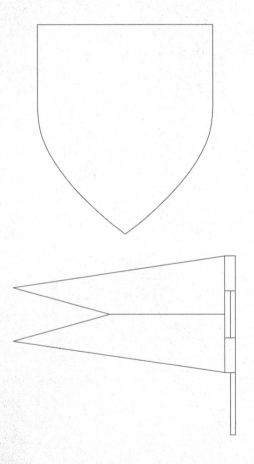

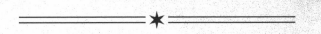

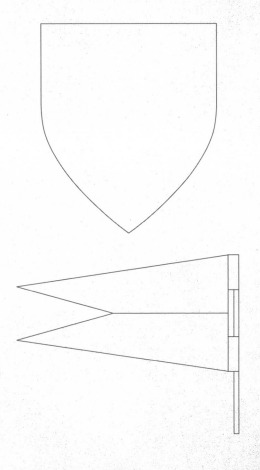

PART FOUR

POSITIONS
& PLAYERS

* * *

"EACH TEAM HAS SEVEN PLAYERS:
THREE CHASERS, TWO BEATERS,
ONE KEEPER, AND A SEEKER."

—Oliver Wood, *Harry Potter and the Sorcerer's Stone*

> "REMEMBER, JUST BECAUSE YOU MADE THE TEAM LAST YEAR, THAT DOESN'T GUARANTEE YOU A SPOT THIS YEAR, IS THAT CLEAR?"
>
> —Harry Potter, *Harry Potter and the Half-Blood Prince*

In *Harry Potter and the Half-Blood Prince*, Harry leads tryouts for Gryffindor's Quidditch team. Ron Weasley tries out for the position of Keeper. For Ron's Quidditch debut, Stuart Craig gave the pitch a different look. He notes, "The trials, the practices, wouldn't have all the colorful fabric. For this we changed it to a sort of skeletal wood form."

Ginny Weasley (Bonnie Wright) rides atop her broomstick wearing her Quidditch uniform. In *Harry Potter and the Half-Blood Prince*, Ginny played the position of Chaser for Team Gryffindor.

★ QUIDDITCH ALL-STARS ★

NAME: Ginny Weasley

NUMBER: 06

POSITION: Chaser/Keeper

★ ★ ★ ★ ★ ★ ★ ★ ★ ★ ★ ★ ★ ★ ★

★ ★ ★ ★ ★ ★ ★ ★ ★ ★ ★ ★ ★ ★ ★

BEATERS

The Beaters use a short wooden bat to whack the Bludger.

★ QUIDDITCH ALL-STARS ★

NAMES: Fred and George Weasley

NUMBERS: 05 and 06

POSITIONS: Beaters

★ ★ ★ ★ ★ ★ ★ ★ ★ ★ ★ ★ ★ ★ ★ ★

★ ★ ★ ★ ★ ★ ★ ★ ★ ★ ★ ★ ★ ★ ★ ★

KEEPER

Cormac McLaggen flies in front of the hoop during Quidditch tryouts. In *Harry Potter and the Half-Blood Prince*, he competed for the position of Keeper against Ron Weasley.

★ ★ ★

"KEEPERS NEED TO BE QUICK, AGILE."

—Ron Weasley, *Harry Potter and the Half-Blood Prince*

★ QUIDDITCH ALL-STARS ★

NAME: Ron Weasley

NUMBER: 02

POSITION: Keeper

★ ★ ★ ★ ★ ★ ★ ★ ★ ★ ★ ★ ★ ★ ★

★ ★ ★ ★ ★ ★ ★ ★ ★ ★ ★ ★ ★ ★ ★

Game play in *Harry Potter and the Half-Blood Prince.*

— ★★★ —

"BUT YOU ARE A SEEKER.
THE ONLY THING I WANT YOU
TO WORRY ABOUT IS THIS...
THE GOLDEN SNITCH."

—Oliver Wood, *Harry Potter and the Sorceror's Stone*

★ QUIDDITCH ALL-STARS ★

NAME: Harry Potter

NUMBER: 07

POSITION: Seeker

★ ★ ★ ★ ★ ★ ★ ★ ★ ★ ★ ★ ★ ★

★ ★ ★ ★ ★ ★ ★ ★ ★ ★ ★ ★ ★ ★

In *Harry Potter and the Prisoner of Azkaban*, Professor Albus Dumbledore (Michael Gambon) rises from the stands during a match between Gryffindor and Hufflepuff. The professor uses a wandless charm to rescue Harry Potter after he falls from his broomstick.

✴ ✴ ✴

"ARRESTO MOMENTUM!"

—Professor Albus Dumbledore,
Harry Potter and the Prisoner of Azkaban

In *Harry Potter and the Half-Blood Prince*, for the first time, fan wear was created for the nonplaying students to support their teams. Costume designer Jany Termime designed track-style T-shirts and hooded sweatshirts with the Hogwarts seal upon one of the four house colors.

QUIDDITCH MAGICAL FILM MOMENTS

I n *Harry Potter and the Deathly Hallows—Part 2*, Lord Voldemort (Ralph Fiennes) and his followers destroyed the Hogwarts Quidditch pitch. During the Battle of Hogwarts, fireballs set the observation towers ablaze and giants uprooted goalposts from the pitch.

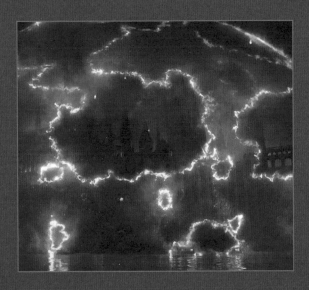

In *Harry Potter and the Sorcerer's Stone*, Madam Hooch (Zoe Wanamaker) serves as the referee during Harry Potter's first Quidditch match.

* * *

"NOW I WANT A NICE, CLEAN GAME—FROM ALL OF YOU!"

—Referee Madam Hooch,
Harry Potter and the Sorcerer's Stone

GAME ON!

Imagine you're a sports writer for *The Daily Prophet*, the wizarding world's most trusted newspaper. Write an article about your favorite Quidditch match of all-time.

_____

_____

_____

_____

_____

_____

_____

_____

_____

_____

_____

_____

_____

_____

_____

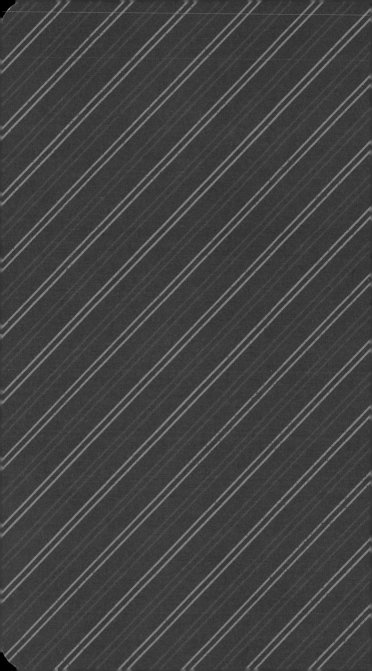

PART FIVE

TOURNAMENTS & TROPHIES

* * *

"AS MINISTER FOR MAGIC,
IT GIVES ME GREAT PLEASURE
TO WELCOME EACH AND EVERY
ONE OF YOU TO THE FINALS OF
THE 422ND QUIDDITCH WORLD CUP.
LET THE MATCH BEGIN!"

—Cornelius Fudge, *Harry Potter and the Goblet of Fire*

The graphic designers on the *Harry Potter and the Goblet of Fire* film created the official flag of the 422nd Quidditch World Cup, a tournament featuring the world's best professional Quidditch teams.

VIKTOR KRUM

A young Quidditch prodigy, Viktor Krum (Stanislav Ianevski) played professionally for the Bulgarian team during the 422nd Quidditch World Cup against the Irish team.

★ ★ ★

"THERE'S NO ONE LIKE KRUM! HE'S LIKE A BIRD THE WAY HE RIDES THE WIND! HE'S MORE THAN AN ATHLETE! HE'S AN ARTIST."

—Ron Weasley, *Harry Potter and the Goblet of Fire*

The prop department referred to the books for inspiration as they created original and altered purchased trophies for the films.

Who will take home the trophy? Fill in your
bracket for the Hogwarts Quidditch Cup.

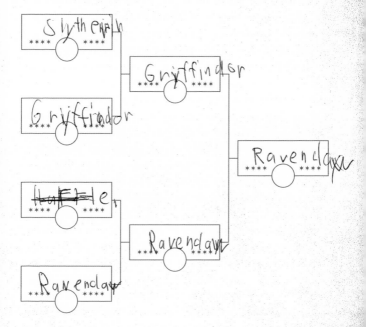

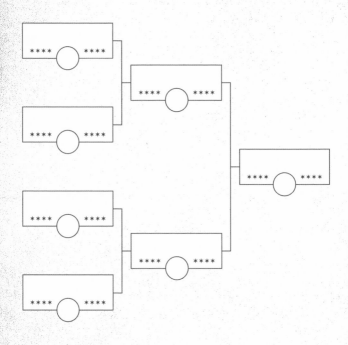

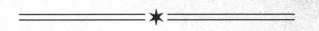

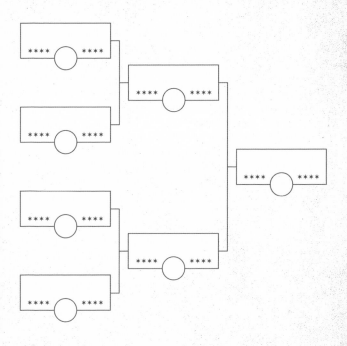

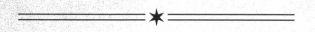

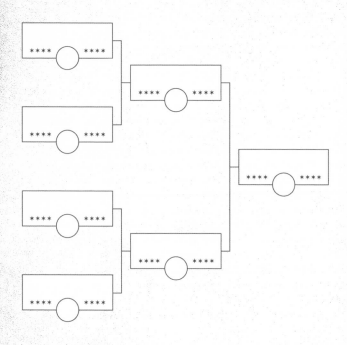

Congratulations!
Add your name to the Quidditch Cup.

PART SIX

YOUR QUIDDITCH PLAYBOOK

Think you can lead a Quidditch team to victory?
Design your own game-winning play. Use Xs to
represent your players and Os for your opponents.

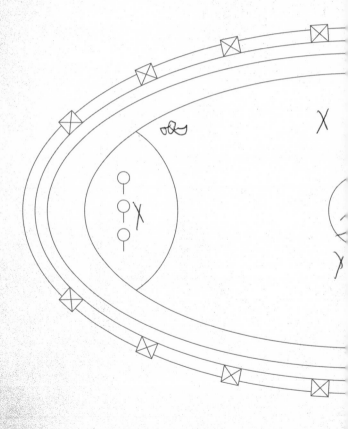

Then draw the best path to carry the Quaffle
(and don't forget about the Golden Snitch)!

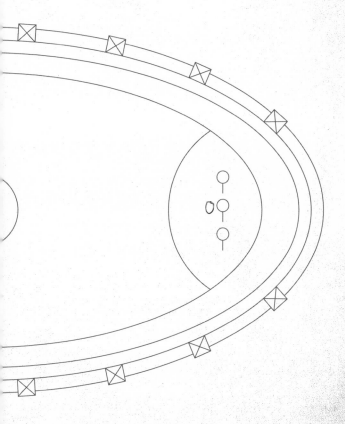

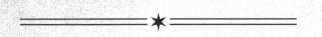

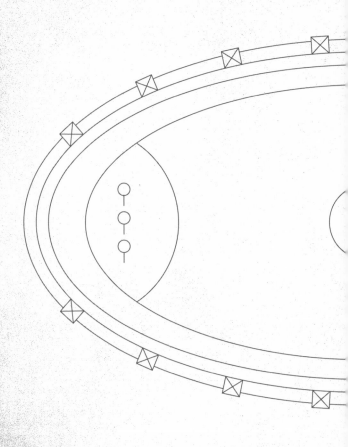

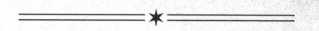

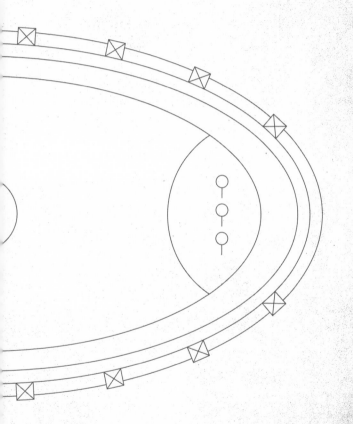

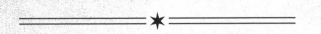

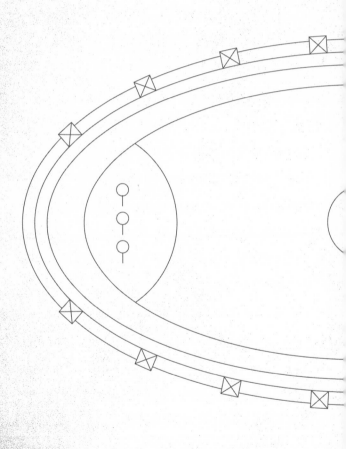

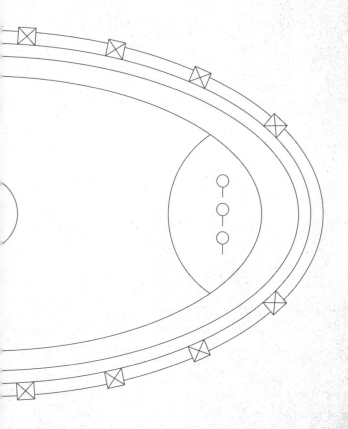

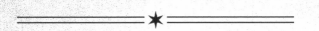

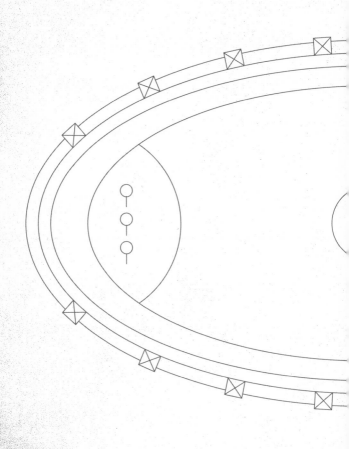

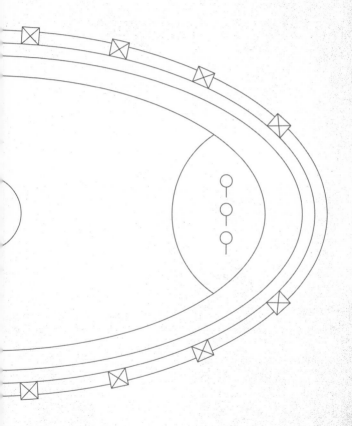

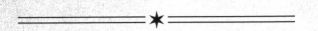

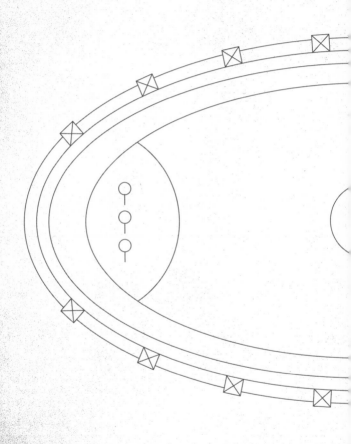

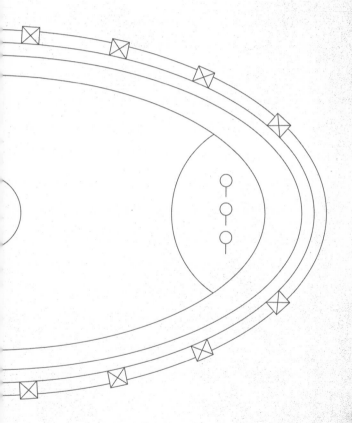

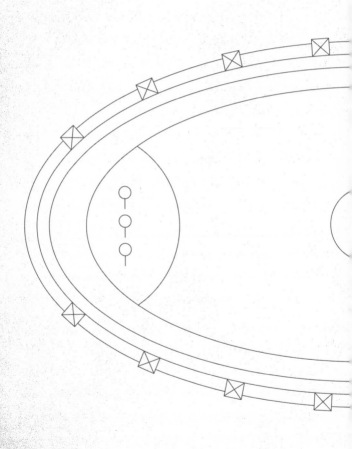

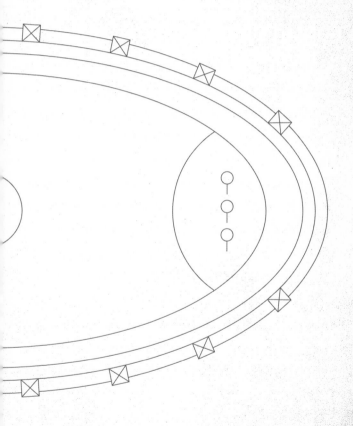

★ NOTES ★

★ NOTES ★

★ NOTES ★

★ NOTES ★

★ NOTES ★

★ NOTES ★

★ NOTES ★